W9-AAB-310

DEAD GUYS TALK

More Wild Willie Mysteries

DEAD GUYS TALK

A WILD WILLIE MYSTERY

BY

BARBARA M. JOOSSE

ILLUSTRATED BY

ABBY CARTER

Clarion Books * New York

Clarion Books
a Houghton Mifflin Company imprint
215 Park Avenue South, New York, NY 10003
Text copyright © 2006 by Barbara M. Joosse
Illustrations copyright © 2006 by Abby Carter

The illustrations were executed in black colored pencil and wash.
The text was set in 14-point Palatino.

www.houghtonmifflinbooks.com

Printed in the U.S.A.

Library of Congress Cataloging-in-Publication Data
Joosse, Barbara M.
Dead guys talk : a Wild Willie mystery / by Barbara M. Joosse ;
illustrated by Abby Carter.
p. cm.
Summary: In the dead middle of summer, the Scarface Detectives
investigate their creepiest case yet when a mysterious client
sends them to Oak Hill Cemetery, where Loonie Loraine is buried.
ISBN-13: 978-0-618-30666-4
ISBN-10: 0-618-30666-8
[1. Cemeteries—Fiction. 2. Detectives—Fiction. 3. Friendship—Fiction.]
I. Carter, Abby, ill. II. Title.
PZ7.J7435Dea 2006
[Fic]—dc22
2005027748

QUM   10 9 8 7 6 5 4 3 2 1

*

For my friend Sarah McEneany, who gets it
—B. M. J.

To Samantha and Carter
—A. C.

*

* CONTENTS *

WANTED: CRIME

HAVE YOU SEEN ANY WEIRD STUFF LATELY?

ARE YOU MISSING ANY JEWELS?

HAS ANYBODY BEEN ACTING UNUSUAL,
LIKE THEY MIGHT COMMIT A CRIME?
REMEMBER—CRIME CAN HAPPEN
ANYTIME, ANYWHERE—EVEN IN
GOOD OLD GRAFTON.

WHEN IT DOES, CALL US.
WE'RE THE CRIME EXPERTS.

* SCARFACE DETECTIVES *

WILD WILLIE

KING KYLE

LUCKY LUCY

(SCARFACE)

* 1 *

Reeks Like Foot Juice

It was the dead middle of summer. At the beginning of summer, there are a million things to do. Building forts, fooling around, solving crimes. At the end, you have to moosh in all the stuff you forgot. But in the middle?

You know what I mean.

Plus, it was hot outside. Really hot. The kind of melty hot where your leg skin sticks together. The kind of hot where your nose breath is the only air that's moving. The kind of hot where you don't like where you are ... but don't want to go where you're not.

One of the reasons my detective partners call me Wild Willie is that I have great ideas. But today? Well, maybe my ideas had boiled in my brain. Because I couldn't think of a single good thing to do.

My best friend, Lucy, and I were drinking soda in my room. We had shoved some of my stuff under the bed so we could sit on the floor. Which is where we were now. Which is where we had been for an hour.

"Willie," said Lucy. "Your room really stinks."

"I know," I said. "There isn't that much to do in here. And this is a really old house. So we don't have air conditioning."

"No," Lucy said. "I don't mean it's a crummy room. I mean it reeks, like foot juice."

"Really?" I said.

"Yuk," said Lucy, holding her nose. "Don't you smell it?"

"I guess not," I said. "Probably I'm used to it."

"Where's the smell coming from?" Lucy sniffed the air and followed the stink trail. Her nose got to the garbage. "Here," she said.

I stuck my nose in there. "Eeew."

"What's in there, anyway?" Lucy asked.

"Well, some tissues with slimy stuff on them. Some sandwiches that are maybe a little moldy. And a banana I found under my bed. I had to scrape it up with my sock. My sock's there, too."

"Aha! Under your bed!" said Lucy.

She lifted the bedspread and looked underneath. Stink blasted out. "WILLIE! THIS IS DISGUSTING! It's even grosser than your garbage. What's under there?"

"I don't exactly know," I said. "But old soccer socks, for sure. And some food. Sometimes when Mom makes liver or fish or vegetarian, I hide it under my bed."

"Oooh," groaned Lucy. "Willie, how often do you clean under there?"

"Clean?" I asked.

"STOP!" said Lucy, holding up her hands. Her face looked green, like mold.

"You don't look so good, Lucy." I opened the window. But it was hot outside, so even the outside smelled rotten. "Maybe we should go someplace that doesn't smell so bad. How about headquarters?"

"Headquarters is in Kyle's attic," Lucy said. "It's a trillion degrees up there."

"Your house?" I asked.

"Forget it. Mom's having a meeting. The women are wearing perfume."

So it seemed like we'd be stuck in my room forever. Boiling, stinky hot. With nothing to do. But sometimes, when you least expect it, opportunity knocks.

Knock knock knock.

"WILLIE!" My other best friend, Kyle, rushed into my room. He was waving an envelope. "Look at this! Somebody sent us something."

The envelope said Scarface Detectives.

"Open it!" I said.

Kyle ripped open the envelope. Inside was a note. It said:

HELP!

And that was all.

"Who's it from?" Lucy asked.

"There's no signature," said Kyle. He looked again at the envelope. "And no return address."

"Hey!" Lucy said. "There's something on the other side of the note."

Kyle flipped the paper over. There was a map on the other side.

It was the dead middle of summer. But an adventure was just beginning.

Did I mention it was dead middle?

* 2 *

x maRkS the . . .

We crammed our heads together and looked at the map. There was an X where we were and an X somewhere else, and a bunch of streets in between.

"Are we supposed to go to the other X spot?" I asked.

"I guess," Kyle said. "Maybe it's like a treasure hunt or something."

Lucy said, "I don't think it's a treasure hunt. The note says 'Help!' Somebody's in trouble."

"Maybe it's a client who needs our detective help," I said.

"Or it could be a trick," Kyle said. "The map doesn't lead to Chuckie's house, does it?"

Chuckie's a kid in the neighborhood. He's bad to the bone. If this was a trick, he'd be behind it. "Noooo," I said, scratching my head. "It's not Chuckie's house. Look." I pointed. "The map leads out of the neighborhood, past the sledding hill, right to the X. So X marks the—"

"CEMETERY!" Lucy said. She let go of the map, and it fluttered to the ground. "The X is smack in the middle of Oak Hill Cemetery."

Kyle picked up the map. "Lucy's right," he said. "That *is* the cemetery." He looked at Lucy and me. "Hey, you guys look pale. You aren't scared of a dumb cemetery, are you?"

"Well, yeah," I said. "Aren't you?"

"Naw," Kyle said. "Cemeteries are just full of a bunch of moldy old dead guys. Dead guys can't hurt you. They're *dead*. But it *is* funny that somebody wants to meet us there."

"Yeah," said Lucy. "Very funny. Ha-ha." She wasn't laughing.

"There's only one way to find out what this is all about. We have to walk to the X. Let's go," said Kyle.

I wanted to go, but my feet seemed stuck to the floor. "You first," I said. "You've got the map."

So Kyle led us outside. We walked past his house, which used to belong to Loony Loraine. When she died, her greedy nephew, Neil, sold it to Kyle's parents. That was Kyle's lucky day. Loraine had been an amateur detective, like us. So her house was full of detective stuff—a secret passage, files full of scoop on everyone in town, detective magazines, and Scarface, a crime-talking parrot.

The neighborhood ended after Kyle's house. You know how it is in a neighborhood. Lots of people recognize you. Lots of people watch you from their windows. If you yelled "HELP!" in your neighborhood, a million moms and dads would come running. But outside of it . . . ? I shivered.

We kept walking. We walked onto Bridge Street . . . over the creek . . . to the sledding hill. Then we saw it:

OAK HILL CEMETERY

There it was, big as life.
Or death.
We followed the map, tiptoeing past

tombstones, fake flowers, trees, and a creepy cement angel. It was getting darker and darker outside. Like somebody was fooling around with the dimmer switch. Finally, we got to the X spot.

It was on an actual grave. "Yowzer!" I said, jumping off. "We're standing on top of a dead guy."

Lucy jumped off, too, but Kyle stayed put. Lucy and I mashed together.

"Whoever's underneath here is D-E-A-D. It's not like he cares. It's not like he can feel us standing here." Kyle danced on top of the grave to prove his point. "La-dee-da-dee-da," he sang. "See? Nothing happened. Nobody jumped up and said 'Boo!' . . . N-n-no bones rattled . . . and n-n-nobody whoooo'd. A dead, putrid, glowing arm did not come out of the ground and g-g-grab me."

Suddenly, Kyle backed off the grave and mashed in with Lucy and me. "I guess it *is* pretty freaky here," he said. "M-m-maybe we should go home."

"Well, we ARE detectives," I said. "We can't give up and walk away just because we're scaredies. We have to snoop around. It's our job. Besides, maybe it *is* Chuckie, playing a trick." I cupped my hand around my mouth. "Hey, Chuckie! We know it's you. Come on out."

But nobody answered. It was still just us and a bunch of dead guys.

"It's not funny, Chuckie!" yelled Lucy. "Come out."

Silence.

"I guess it's not Chuckie," Kyle said. "If it was, he'd be laughing his head off now, calling us suckers."

"Let's keep investigating." I circled the grave. On the other side was a weird-looking tree. It was huge. And bumpy, like it had warts. And the roots stuck out of the grass like bony toes. There was a giant hole in it that looked like a screaming mouth.

"Hey!" I said. Next to the mouth hole was our next clue. "Another note!" We crammed together to read it. It said:

This is the place.

Lucy snatched it off the tree. Like before, there was writing on the other side. It said:

Somebody's trying to
sell the cemetery.
We don't want to move.
We need your help!
Come back for further
communication.

"Oh, man!" Kyle whispered.
I thought the dark and the map and the

note and the cemetery and the skeleton tree were as creepy as things could get. I thought, *If this were a scary movie, this would be the worst part. Now things will get better.* Only they didn't. Things got creepier, because that's when we read the writing on the tombstone. It said:

Loraine Lamonde,
beloved aunt of Neil.
May she rest in peace.

* 3 *

one BIG MONSteR

"Yow! This is Loony Loraine's grave!" I said.

"And I *danced* on it," said Kyle.

We backed up, one shaky step at a time. Farther and farther . . .

Right into bony arms!

"AAAAAIGH!" we yelled.

"Hey," Lucy said. "It's just a bunch of vines." She shook a stem. "See?"

"Right," I said. "A vine."

Kyle shivered. "It's no wonder we're creeped out. We're in a *cemetery!* It's spooky to walk on dead people's graves. And we haven't even met our client. Why isn't our client here, anyway?"

I looked around. "Maybe she is," I whispered.

"You don't mean . . . ?" said Kyle, looking over his shoulder. *Rumble.*

". . . that our client's . . . a ghost?" I whispered. A shiver ran down my back. "Maybe."

Rumble rumble.

"Is s-s-somebody grumbling?" Kyle asked. "Willie? Is that you?"

Crack!

"It's thunder," said Lucy. "It's going to storm!" *Split, splat.* "Here it comes. Let's run for it!"

We started to run.

The sky growled at us: *grumble grumble grumble.* The sky cracked at us. *SNAP!*

The water—*split, splat*—started coming faster and faster. Suddenly:

Whooooooosh!

"Yowzer!" I yelled. "It's pouring!"

We ran faster. My heart bashed around in my chest and my legs burned like crazy, but I kept running. All of a sudden, it felt like everything mooshed together and turned into one big monster—the thunder, the lightning, the skeleton tree, the bony vine, the dead people in the cemetery, and Loony Loraine. I ran and ran and ran . . . like I was running for my life.

Mom was drinking coffee in the living room. "Goodness!" she said. "You're soaking wet. And white as sheets. Would you like some cocoa?"

Mom wrapped us in towels and warmed the milk.

Sometimes I think orphans are lucky. They don't have moms to bug them. There's nobody to make you do chores. Nobody to tell you to do your homework. Nobody to say, "Pick up your room and DON'T forget under the bed. Are you listening to me?"

But this wasn't one of those times.

Mom mixed the cocoa and squirted big mounds of whipped cream on top. She set the mugs in front of us, along with a bowl of salted peanuts in the shell. Then she went back to the living room.

I sipped my cocoa and sprayed a whipped-cream mustache on my face. "Yowzer," I said, through the mustache.

"No kidding," said Lucy. "That cemetery sure was spooky." She squirted herself whipped-cream eyebrows.

"After we got the note, *everything* was spooky. I kept getting goose bumps, but it was hot outside. I kept feeling that someone was watching us, but no one was there."

"Maybe it was the storm coming," Kyle said. He cracked open a nut. "There's a lot of electricity in the air before a storm. Electricity-air can give you goose bumps."

"That could have been it," said Lucy. "Almost for sure."

"Read the second note again," said Kyle.

Lucy unfolded the soaking-wet note carefully and read it out loud.

"What does it mean?" Kyle asked. "*Who's* trying to sell the cemetery? What happens to all the dead bodies when a cemetery is sold? Do they throw them in the garbage? Do they put them in another cemetery?"

"And do we get a reward if we solve the case? And what exactly IS the case?" added Lucy. "This is not your usual mystery."

Kyle popped a nut into his mouth. "How can we figure out the case if we don't know who our client is?"

"We need to surveil," Lucy said. "We need

to watch the cemetery, to see who comes and goes. Maybe we'll catch somebody leaving a note on Loony Loraine's grave. Then we'll know that's our client."

"But what if our client *is* a ghost?" I asked.

"Think about it. Those dead guys are nice and cozy in their graves. The note said: 'WE DON'T WANT TO MOVE.' Plus—and this is a very big plus—the second note was on Loony Loraine's personal grave."

"You mean . . . Loony Loraine is our client?" Kyle asked.

"I'm not saying she is. And I'm not saying she's not," I said.

"We have to consider all possibilities," said Lucy. "Loony Loraine might be our client. Or maybe it's somebody alive. Really, it could be anybody. We'll just have to stay alert."

The doorbell rang.

"Maybe that's our client now," Kyle said, running for the door. He swung it open.

There wasn't anybody there.

* 4 *

SURveiLLance

I woke up the next morning and snapped the shade up. The storm had blasted the heat out of the air. It was clear. You could see a mile away. It was great weather for surveillance, and I had a plan.

After breakfast, I gathered up supplies and rode my bike to headquarters. I rang Kyle's doorbell and went in. Then I walked into Kyle's room . . . into his closet . . . behind his clothes . . . through the secret passage . . . to headquarters.

"*Man oh man oh man,*" Scarface said in

Loraine's exact voice. Scarface is an African Grey. African Greys are the world's smartest parrots. Scarface knows a million words, most of them detective words. Loraine taught her to talk, so she sounds just like her.

She paced back and forth on the desk like a short, feathered detective. *"Murder. Missing jewels. Stick 'em up,"* she muttered.

I was wearing my yesterday shorts and there were some peanuts in the pockets. I held a few out to Scarface.

"Braaack! Scarface want some?" she said, hopping around on the desk. *"Want some, want some?"* Peanuts are Scarface's favorite food. She took the peanuts and started chomping.

"Hi-ho," I said to Lucy and Kyle.

"Everybody's here," said Lucy. "Let's make plans. We have to observe the cemetery, but we don't want to be watched. We don't know who our client is, and we want to find out."

Kyle, Lucy, and Scarface looked at me. I *am* the Idea Man, after all.

"Here's the plan," I said. "We sneak to the cemetery. Kyle and Lucy, you can cover. You watch from the sledding hill. You can see great from up there. I'll walk into the cemetery and look around. Then I'll set up a trap."

"*Gotcha!*" said Scarface.

"A trap?" asked Kyle.

"The note said, 'Come back for further communication.' That means, somehow, our client has to get back to the grave to leave another note. Here comes the trap part. I brought some sewing thread. It's really thin. You can hardly see it. See?" I took the spool out of my pocket. "So I wind this all over Loony Loraine's grave. Later, if there's another note from our client, we check the thread. If it's been moved, then we know a regular person has walked on the grave. If it hasn't . . ."

"Then our client's a ghost?" whispered

Kyle. "Because ghosts don't have actual bodies. They can't move thread."

"Brilliant," said Lucy.

"Of course," I said.

"We need disguises for surveillance," Kyle said.

"You and Lucy could see the cemetery better with binoculars," I said. "Can binoculars be part of your disguise?"

"We could be birdwatchers!" said Lucy. "They're snoopy, and they sit around with notebooks and binoculars."

"Yes!" said Kyle. "We could pretend we're having a picnic on the sledding hill and watching for birds. But what do birdwatchers wear?"

"Dorky stuff," said Lucy. "Like this!"

Lucy has a big box of disguises that she donated to the agency. She reached in the box and pulled out:

wigs
shade hats

khaki stuff
a shirt with an alligator on it
one fake mustache

Kyle got out the binoculars and another notebook. "And this part is perfect," he said. "My dad's got a birdwatcher's guide. We can take that along."

"Willie, why don't you wear a football player's disguise?" said Lucy. She handed

me a uniform and shoulder pads. "You won't look like you. And the padding will make you look like you have muscles. It might scare off bad guys."

"I do have muscles," I said, flexing. "But I'll wear the pads anyway."

After I was dressed, I looked at myself in the mirror. I looked great. I guess fake muscles is the reason guys become football players.

"We're ready to rock and roll," said Lucy.

We split up. Kyle and Lucy walked ahead. I walked behind (to see if they were being followed). I looked at reflections in the window (to see if I was being followed). I bent over to tie my shoe (to check for anybody suspicious). I crossed the street (to see if anyone crossed with me).

The coast was clear.

Kyle and Lucy climbed up the sledding hill across from the cemetery. Then they set up a picnic—a blanket over the ground, food on top of that. Kyle got out the birdwatcher's guide. Lucy got out the binoculars. They were all set.

Now it was my turn. I leaned against a lamppost. Ho-hum. I stretched. I looked around. I tied my shoe. I crossed the street again. Nobody was following. Ready, set, . . .

Go! I climbed the path to the cemetery. I opened the metal gate—*creeaak!*—and went inside. Alone. Now it was just me and the dead guys. I was glad Lucy and Kyle were watching me with the binoculars.

I headed for Loraine's grave. I swiveled my head around, watching for anything unusual. But all the time I felt like I was *being* watched. I felt alone in the cemetery, but *not* alone. Could dead people see you from under the ground? Or did they float on top? Was I walking through their invisible bodies?

And here's the thing. If you're dead and invisible, you'd be the world's sneakiest detective.

I observed. There was a small building at the far end of the cemetery. A shed? I hadn't noticed it yesterday. I kept walking and eyeballed the tombstones. They were really old. Some were leaning and some were broken. I read the names, and this is what I noticed: *A lot of the names were Lamonde!* Wow! Dead Lamondes were all over the place.

Finally, I got to Loraine's grave. I got the thread out of my pocket and wound it all around. I was busy winding string from a fake flower to the tree when suddenly someone yelled, "ARE YOU LOOKING FOR SOMETHING?"

* 5 *

BIG VOICE

Whoa! I jerked my head up. A man was standing there. A huge man.

"Huh?" I said.

"ARE YOU LOOKING FOR SOME-THING?" said the deep, loud voice.

"N-n-no," I said. "L-L-Loraine was my neighbor. I just came for a visit."

"LORAINE WAS A GOOD LADY," said the voice. He sounded like he was yelling through a tunnel.

Loraine had practically been a hermit. She hardly left her house. She hardly let anybody

inside. So how did Big Voice know about her? "Did you know her?" I asked.

"I KNOW EVERYBODY IN HERE," said Big Voice. "I TAKE CARE OF THEM."

"Y-y-you do?" I asked.

"YES. THEY'RE MY FRIENDS."

Big Voice, friends with the dead guys? Yowzer! "Gotta be going," I said. I jumped off Loraine's grave.

"COME BACK SOON!" yelled Big Voice.

I ran out of the cemetery. Big Voice yelled from behind, "DON'T BE A STRANGER!"

I ran like crazy. My good old partners were waiting for me on the picnic blanket. I dove onto the blanket—*splatt!*—right onto a pile of chips.

"Willie!" Lucy said. "Who was yelling at you?"

"Big Voice," I said, picking little pieces of chips out of my hair. "I don't know his real name. But he wasn't exactly yelling *at* me. He was just yelling."

"Just somebody loud, then," said Kyle, nodding. "Like Scarface."

"He's weird, though," I said.

"Let's see what he's up to." Lucy looked through the binoculars. "Hmm," she said. "Willie, you'd better write this down."

I flipped open the cover of our detective notebook. "Ready," I said.

"The subject is walking to a little shed," Lucy said.

I wrote that down. I wondered: *What's in the shed? Dead bodies? Live ones?*

"He's putting a key into a padlock, and now he's turning it," said Lucy. "He's opening the shed door . . . and taking out a bushel basket. Now he's picking up sticks, and putting them in the basket."

"He's cleaning up the cemetery after the storm. Big Voice must the groundskeeper," said Kyle.

After a while, Big Voice took the basket to the curb and went back and locked up the shed. Then he walked away, swinging a lunch bucket. He was whistling.

"So what's the story on Big Voice?" asked Lucy.

"What did he say to you in the cemetery?" asked Kyle.

"You mean, what did he *yell* to me," I said.
"He yelled that Loraine was a nice lady. That
he knew everybody in the cemetery. That he
took care of them. And that they were his
friends."

"Hmm," said Kyle. "That *is* weird."

"Maybe you have to be weird to work in a
cemetery," Lucy said.

I continued my report. "I set up the trap.
We can inspect it after lunch, to see if it's
been disturbed," I said. "And one more
thing. I checked out the tombstones. There
are a whole lot of Lamondes buried in
there."

"That's Loraine's last name," said Lucy.
"Veeeery interesting."

"No kidding," I said. "They might as well
call it Lamonde Cemetery."

* 6 *

MR. BRIEFCASE

"Hey, I didn't know the cemetery was such a popular place. Here comes a big black car," Lucy said.

A fancy car pulled in through the gate. "Maybe it's a hearse," I said, "with a coffin inside."

"No, hearses are a different shape," said Kyle. "This is just a rich guy's car. Maybe he's visiting a dead relative." Kyle looked through the binoculars. "The rich guy's wearing shiny shoes, and he's carrying a briefcase. And a long tube."

"Look," said Lucy. "He's bending over somebody's grave. Yup. He's visiting a relative."

I looked through the binoculars. "Then how come he's taking the flowers *out* of the vase?" I asked.

"He's probably going to put fresh ones in," said Kyle. "You know. For the dead guy."

"Wow. He must have a lot of dead relatives because now he's going to someone else's grave. And look! He's taking out those flowers, too," I said.

After he took flowers from two more graves, Lucy said, "Mr. Briefcase is stealing flowers from dead guys! What a slime!"

Exactly at that moment, another car pulled in behind Mr. Briefcase. A lady got out. *And Mr. Briefcase gave her the flowers!*

"What a creep," Kyle said. He looked through the binoculars again. "Now Mr. Briefcase is showing Ms. Flowers some stuff in his briefcase. Papers. Now he's pulling a long piece of paper out of the tube. He's unrolling it. They're looking at the big paper together, and she's pointing. Now he's taking another paper out of his briefcase . . . and she's signing it."

After that, Mr. Briefcase and Ms. Flowers got back in their cars and left the cemetery.

"What was that all about?" I said.

"I don't know," said Lucy. "But something stinks."

OooooooOOOOOOOO! It was the noon whistle. It was time to go home for lunch. I ditched the football pads and gave them to Kyle to take to headquarters. We flicked the smooshed chips off the blanket and headed home. On the way, I had the same watching-me feeling.

Was that movement? I swiveled my head around, but nothing was there. Was that breathing? No, just the wind. Were those footsteps? Just mine. Still . . .

Mom was in the kitchen, heating up soup. I lifted the lid to see what kind. Cheesy cheddar, my favorite. Mom spooned some into a bowl. I breathed in the soup smell.

"How's the case going?" Mom asked.

Should I tell her that this was the creepiest case we'd ever had? That we were surveilling in a cemetery and that a weird guy yelled at me and that we had a client who might be dead? Should I mention that I kept having a shivery feeling, like someone was watching me?

Would you?

"Fine," I said, and took a spoonful of soup.

"Who's your client?" Mom asked.

"I can't tell you. It's confidential."

"Naturally," said Mom. "What's the mystery you have to solve, then?"

"Sorry," I said. "Confidential."

"Oh," Mom said. "I guess the whole thing is confidential, then."

"Yup."

"Just as long as you're home in time for dinner." Mom scruffled my hair. She picked out a chip piece. "A new hair product?" she asked, holding up the chip.

"Yes," I said. "It's for texture."

* 7 *

ᏴOᎠᎽᎶᏌᎪᎡᎠ ᏚᎬᎡᏙᏆᏟᎬ

At headquarters, there were clothes and wigs everywhere. "More disguises?" I asked.

"Yes," Lucy said. "We're going back to the cemetery to check the thread. We don't want anyone to recognize our old disguises."

"Yowzer," I said. "This is getting complicated."

"I know," said Lucy. "But safety first."

I put on a Chicago Cubs cap. I put on a brand-name T-shirt. I put on sunglasses. I looked like a Chicago city kid.

Kyle put on a nerd costume—plastic

pocket protector, fake glasses with duct tape, a weird shirt. Lucy put on a girlie-girl outfit—a dress with a swirly skirt and shoes with bows on them.

"*Hubba-hubba,*" said Scarface to Lucy.

"Wow!" said Kyle, as Lucy turned around. "You sure don't look like you."

"Thank you," said Lucy.

We looked in the mirror. "Nobody will ever guess it's us," I said.

"Then let's adios," said Lucy.

"This is really a creepy case," I said as we walked outside. I picked up a big stick.

"No kidding," said Kyle, snapping off a thorny branch. "Cemeteries and ghosts and nut cases. I wouldn't mind a little protection."

"Yeah. Something so big and bad it would scare off anything," Lucy said, grabbing a rock.

"Even weirdos," said Kyle.

"Or ghosts," said Lucy.

"If there are such things," I said.

As we walked, I heard the breathing-footsteps thing again. I saw the moving shadows. This time I was positive. *It wasn't the wind. It wasn't my imagination. Somebody was following us.*

I flipped open my notebook and wrote: "I think somebody's following us. Do you?" Then I passed the note to my partners. Kyle and Lucy both nodded. We were walking next to the big dark hedgerow when suddenly . . .

Sproing!

It was Chuckie. "Well. . . . If it isn't Scarface Detectives."

"How did you know it's us?" said Kyle. "We're wearing disguises."

"You can't fool a fooler," said Chuckie. "Where are you going?"

"We're on a case," Kyle said.

"I see you're carrying sticks and rocks. I guess you're scared of something. Need some help?" Chuckie asked. He reached in his pocket and whipped out a business card. It said:

CHUCKIE'S BODYGUARD SERVICE

* 24-HOUR PROTECTION *

* 24-HOUR PEACE OF MIND *

"Bodyguard service?" Kyle asked.

"The world is full of creeps and pervs. I'm big and I'm rotten. I scare everybody," Chuckie said.

"This isn't a free service, though, is it?" I asked.

"Of course not," said Chuckie. "I *am* a businessman."

"A low-down crook is more like it," said

Lucy. "Which is exactly what we *don't* need. Get lost."

There are only two people in the entire universe who can say "Get lost" to the Chuckster. His mother and Lucy. Chuckie's mother can say it because she feeds him. Lucy can say it because Chuckie used to be in love with her. Maybe he still is.

"I can take the hint," said Chuckie. "I'll make like a tree and leave." He hopped on his dirt bike and started to pedal away.

He had almost disappeared when Lucy yelled, "Wait!"

Chuckie screeched on the brakes and came back. He was grinning.

I sighed. "How much?" I asked.

Chuckie popped three purple jawbreakers into his mouth. All at the same time. The jawbreakers clacked around in his mouth like breaking bones. "Mrklbrkl?" Chuckie mumbled.

"Chuckie, we can't understand you with your mouth full," Lucy said.

Chuckie spit the jawbreakers into his

hand. They floated around like three purple heads in a lake of purple slime. He said, "This is the consultation. This is the free part. After that, it's a dollar per person per diem."

"THREE DOLLARS A DAY?" Lucy asked.

"No. A dollar for Willie. A dollar for Kyle." He smiled again. "But I won't charge you, Lucille. You're on the house."

"We need to conference," I said.

"Alone," Lucy said.

"Make it quick," said Chuckie. "This is still the free part."

We huddled.

"I have a bad feeling about this," I said. "This could be a setup. Maybe Chuckie's just making us scared so he can cash in."

"But if the case is for real, Chuckie *would* make a great bodyguard," Lucy said.

"Two bucks a day is expensive, but maybe we can solve the case in a couple of days," Kyle said. "Then it wouldn't cost so much."

"I'd really like 24-hour peace of mind," I said.

"And I'll chip in," said Lucy. "Even though I'm actually free."

I still had a bad feeling about hiring Chuckie, but I turned around. "Okay, Chuckie. You're hired."

"You won't be sorry," said Chuckie cheerfully. "*Everybody's* afraid of me. Who's after you, anyway?" Chuckie popped the jawbreakers back in his mouth one by one. He wiped his hand on his shorts.

"We don't know if anyone's after us or not," said Kyle. "We're hiring you just in case."

"Just stick with us and don't ask questions," said Lucy.

"Wmy wlips are wsealed," Chuckie said. He tried to close his lips, to demonstrate. But he couldn't get his mouth around the jawbreakers. A little purple drool dribbled down his chin.

* 8 *

Some Slimeball

Chuckie slurped his jawbreakers and stomped his feet on the sidewalk. He crossed his arms over his chest. He was big. He was mean. He was bad.

Here's the good part: Big old Chuckie would scare the bad guys off.

Here's the bad part: Hiring Chuckie was like having a pet rattlesnake. You never knew when the worm would turn.

"What are we doing in a cemetery?" Chuckie asked when we got there.

Kyle, Lucy, and I looked at one another.

How much should we tell Chuckie? He was our paid bodyguard, but the less he knew, the better.

Lucy said, "No offense, Chuckie, but we can't tell you everything. We're in the cemetery because our case is here."

"You mean your client?" Chuckie said.

"Uh . . . we don't actually know who our client is. But we get messages here," Kyle said.

"How come he leaves messages in a cemetery?" asked Chuckie.

"We don't know," I said. "But the case we're on has something to do with the cemetery."

"Let me get this straight," Chuckie said. "You have a mysterious client who you've never seen with your eyeballs. And your case has something to do with the cemetery. Ghost work, huh? And I thought you guys were weenies."

What was Chuckie, anyway? A wizard? How did he worm all that out of us?

When we got to Loraine's grave, we checked out the thread. It was still up.

We circled the grave. "There isn't a note," Kyle said. "And nobody's torn down the thread, so nobody's been here. Now what?"

I said, "I guess we'll come back tomorrow, then."

"WAIT!" Chuckie held up his hands. "There was a note here before?"

We nodded.

"Where?"

"Tacked to the tree," I said.

"What if your client put the note somewhere else, close by?" Chuckie said.

"Like where?" Lucy asked.

"I have an idea," Chuckie said, slurping his jawbreakers. "But so far you're only paying for bodyguard services. Not idea services."

"CHUCKIE!" Lucy said.

"I *am* a businessman. But I like to see my customers satisfied. How about this arrangement? If I find a note, you pay a dollar. If I don't, my idea is on the house."

"Deal," I said.

Chuckie reached into the hole in the tree. "Pay dirt," he said.

How did Chuckie think of looking in the tree hole? Something was definitely fishy.

Chuckie pulled out a newspaper. An article was circled in red:

SHOPPING CENTER
TO BE BUILT

The Grafton Chamber of Commerce announced that a new shopping center will be built next year in Grafton. The enclosed mall, to be named La Malle, will be built on the corner of Bridge and Oak Streets. Construction will begin next April and will be completed the following year.

A spokesperson for Double L Investments announced six retail businesses will occupy the space—Food Market, Fry Guy, the Office Place, Mona's Threads, House of Kurl, and In Sense Perfumes.

The property is currently Oak Hill Cemetery, a small privately owned cemetery. Most of the graves are very old. The bodies will be relocated to the larger Grafton Cemetery prior to construction.

Kyle poked at the newspaper. "That's it! The cemetery's being sold to make room for a shopping center! Who's the slimeball who's moving all the dead bodies?"

Lucy slapped her hand to her head. "Hey! I just thought of something. Remember that long tube Mr. Briefcase was carrying? Remember when he pulled rolled-up papers out and showed them to the lady? I know what those papers were—*blueprints*."

"Yeah!" said Kyle, hopping around. "You use blueprints when you build something. Like a house—"

"OR A SHOPPING CENTER!" I said. "I bet those were blueprints for the shopping center!"

"In that case, Mr. Briefcase is Mr. Slime-ball," Kyle said.

"He-he-he." Chuckie grinned like a cheesy salesman. "This caper keeps getting better and better," he said.

"Our client said, 'We don't want to move.' She wants us to stop the sale," I said.

"If you were dead . . . and you were buried, all nice and cozy . . . and you were used to your place . . . and maybe you even had neighbors you liked who were buried there, too . . . then you wouldn't want to move. Right?" Lucy said.

"Right," Kyle said. "Nobody likes to move." He looked at the article again. "Who's Double L Investments anyway? And it says that the cemetery is privately owned. Who owns it? And who's Mr. Slimeball?"

"YOU'RE BACK AGAIN!" came a big, loud voice. "I KNEW YOU'D BE BACK."

* 9 *

Something About that name . . .

I spun around, and there was Big Voice. In the creepy-crawly flesh.

Chuckie stood square in front of Lucy.

"AND I SEE YOU BROUGHT YOUR FRIENDS," said Big Voice.

"Y-y-yes," I said.

"CAN YOU STAY A WHILE? I HAVE SOME COOKIES IN MY LUNCH BUCKET. WE COULD HAVE A PICNIC. I'M *DYING* FOR A PICNIC. HE-HE. THAT'S A LITTLE CEMETERY HUMOR." Big Voice dangled his metal lunch bucket in front of our faces and smiled. His smile didn't have fangs in it, which at least was something.

"Well, uh, it's nice of you to ask," said Lucy. "But I hear my dad calling us." She pretended to listen for something. "Yup. That's Dad all right. Big bad Dad. Did I mention my dad is a karate expert?" Lucy pretended to listen again. She yelled over her shoulder, "We're coming, Dad. We'll be right there." She turned to Big Voice. "Gotta go!"

Then we ran out of the cemetery. Chuckie hung behind, protecting our rear. We met him outside the gate.

Chuckie said, "Who was that loud guy? A pervert?"

"We're not sure," said Kyle. "But we think he's the groundskeeper for the cemetery."

"Wow," said Chuckie. "Ghosts and pervs. Where are we going now?"

"To headqua . . ." I started to say. But I didn't want Chuckie to know.

"Oh," Chuckie said. "You're going to headquarters at Kyle's?"

I sighed. "Yeah."

When we got there, Kyle said, "Chuckie, you can go home now. We don't need your services here."

"Okay. But you still owe me for a whole day," Chuckie said.

"Yes," I said.

"Another day, another dollar," said Chuckie, and he left.

"*Hands up, scumbag,*" said Scarface when we got upstairs to headquarters.

"Hi, Scarface," Kyle said.

"Let's review," I said, taking out my notebook. "What do we know?"

"Well, now we know the reason the cemetery is being sold. We think the scumbag is Mr. Briefcase. We need to find out who Mr. Briefcase and Double L Investments are," Lucy said.

I took notes.

"And, of course, we still don't know who our client is," Kyle said.

"Loraine was an amateur detective. We've had two communications right at her grave. And there's that creepy feeling, like someone is watching us, maybe her ghost."

"Maybe you're right about being watched," Lucy said. "But maybe the 'watcher' is somebody alive. Don't you think it's funny that Chuckie was waiting for us when we got out of headquarters? Like he knew we'd be creeped out? Do you think Chuckie's the one who's been following us all along?"

"And think about this," Kyle said. "How did Chuckie know to look in that tree for the newspaper?"

"Willie, what's Chuckie's tab?" asked Lucy.

I turned to the finance page. "We owe Chuckie two dollars for today and a dollar for an idea. So three bucks."

"Chuckie gets two dollars a day, PLUS he charges for ideas. If I know Chuckie, he's going to have lots of ideas," Lucy said.

"Maybe it's Chuckie's scam," I said. "But it sure felt great to have big old Chuckie watching our rear in the cemetery with Big Voice and all those creepy graves."

Lucy and Kyle nodded.

"Let's investigate . . . and keep our eye on Chuckie at the same time," I said.

"Okay," Kyle said. "Let's look at the newspaper again." We crammed our heads together.

"There's something about that article," Lucy said. "Something smells fishy."

"What do you mean?" I asked.

"I'm not sure." She looked at the article again. "Something about the name of the mall, La Malle."

"It's a stupid name," said Kyle. "But shopping centers usually have stupid names."

"No, not that," she said. "Something about the name. . . . It rings a bell."

Ding-dong.

"Hello. Come in. Hello hello," said Scarface.

It was the doorbell.

* 10 *

WIZARD OF WORM

We rushed to the front door.

"*Yer under arrest!*" said Scarface as Chuckie burst in.

"*I smell a rat,*" said Scarface.

"Hey!" said Chuckie. "That parrot's a regular blabbermouth."

"*Blabbermouth. Blab blab blabbermouth,*" Scarface repeated.

"Chuckie," Lucy said. "What are you doing here? We told you to go home."

"I know," said Chuckie. "I did. But then I had a brainstorm. Let's get to headquarters and I'll tell you the scoop."

Man, I sure didn't like the way this was going down. Chuckie was horning in on our case. He was taking over *and* he was making loot. "Not so fast," I said. "Headquarters is only for detectives."

"How come?" Chuckie asked.

"There's . . . uh . . . a lot of delicate information there," I said.

"Right," Kyle said. "Confidential information. We'd like to let you up there, but we can't. Anyway, what's the scoop?"

"He-he. Let's just say I have some delicate information of my own. Let's just say"—he sang this part—"I know something you don't know."

"*I know something you don't know,*" Scarface sang.

"Then spill," said Lucy.

"Remember when you said to seal my lips? Well, the thing is, once a person's lips are sealed, it's hard to open them."

"You mean, it's expensive," said Lucy.

"Exactly," said Chuckie.

"How expensive?" I asked.

"I think of it like this. Little bits of information are cheap. Big bits are expensive. But this information is MONGO." He held out his hand. "Ten bucks."

Lucy shot arrow-eyes at Chuckie. "Forget it," she said. "There's no way we're going to pay that much. Anyway, how do we know it's mongo information?"

"Take my word for it," Chuckie said.

"Five bucks if it's mongo, nothing if it's not. Take it or leave it," I said.

"Take it," Chuckie said. "I found out who Double L Investments is," he whispered. We had to lean in to hear him. His breath smelled like taco chips.

"WHO?" we said at once.

"A guy named Neil Lamonde."

"Neil! Loraine's greedy nephew!" cried Lucy. "He's the one who sold her house to Kyle's mom and dad . . . while Loraine's dead body was practically still warm. Of course! He'd be the weasely scumbag with his fingers in the pot."

"Then Neil is Mr. Briefcase!" I yelled. "The guy who stole dead people's flowers at the cemetery. What a dirty rat!"

"*Neil's a dirty rat. Dirty rat dirty rat dirty rat,*" Scarface repeated.

"And that's why the name of the shopping center rang a bell," Lucy said. "Because La Malle sounds like Lamonde."

"Chuckie, how did you get this information?" I asked.

"I know all, I see all," said Chuckie.

"*I know all, I see all,*" Scarface repeated.

"I asked around until I found somebody who knew who Double L Investments was. I can worm information out of anybody," Chuckie said cheerfully. "I have a gift."

That was Chuckie, all right. The Wizard of Worm. The question is, *Had the worm turned?* Was Chuckie ripping us off?

Chuckie thumped a thick finger into my chest. "Willie, don't forget to put five more bucks on the tab."

I wrote down $5. Chuckie was already getting $8, and it was only the first day. PLUS he was horning in on our business.

"What do we do next?" asked Kyle.

"I could pound Neil," said Chuckie helpfully. He cracked his knuckles. "It would be so much fun, I wouldn't even charge. It would be on the house."

"Chuckie! You can't go around pounding people," Lucy said.

"Why not?" he asked.

"He's a grownup, for one thing," I said.

"It's against the law," said Kyle. "You could be arrested."

"Plus, it isn't nice. There are other ways to solve problems, you know," said Lucy.

"Maybe," said Chuckie. "But pounding has always worked for me. Anyway, what other ways are there?"

"Interrogation. Surveillance. Plans," I said. "To name a few."

"See, Chuckie, when it comes to plans, Willie's the expert," Kyle said. "He's probably already thought of a way to get Neil to leave the cemetery alone. Right, Willie?"

"Uh . . . right!" Actually, I didn't have a plan. I had a headache. But maybe my head hurt because there was a plan in there. Any minute the plan would pop out. Then my headache would be gone. And La Malle would be history. And we would have solved the world's greatest case.

And best of all? *I'd* be the hero. Not Chuckie, the Wizard of Worm.

* 11 *

pop!

I'm the Idea Man. The team expected a brilliant idea out of me. And Chuckie would laugh his head off if I didn't have one. I needed a plan to stop the sale. A big, fat, foolproof, brilliant plan.

That night, I put my notebook next to the bed. I opened it up to a blank page and put a pencil there. I went to sleep and waited for inspiration.

In the morning, the page was still empty.

After breakfast, we went to the cemetery—Kyle, Scarface, Chuckie, Lucy, and me.

"Y-y-you do?" asked Neil. His voice was shaky. "What do you know? Do you know about the tax scam? The forgery? The gambling? What?"

Wow. Neil did all that?

"Tax scam. Forgery. Gambling," Scarface repeated. *"Gotcha!"*

"Auntie! Please!" Neil whined. "I'll get in trouble if you blab."

"Blabbermouth blabbermouth."

"This is a small town. If you blab, everything will be plastered in the newspaper. All my customers will think I'm a rat. I'll be ruined. I could even go to jail!"

"*Neil's a dirty rat. Dirty rat dirty rat dirty rat.*"

Neil crumbled to his knees. "Come on, Auntie. Come ON!" He started blubbering. He was practically drowning in blubber.

He wiped his nose on his sleeve and said, "Okay. You win. I'll call off the shopping center deal."

Neil dragged himself up. He slumped away, slowly at first. Then he started running like crazy.

We skidded down the hill so we could get a good look at his smarmy face. On the sidewalk, Neil almost smashed into Chuckie.

"Hey, buddy," said Chuckie. "Is something wrong? You look like you've seen a ghost or something."

Neil jumped in his car and squealed away.

The dust settled. A crow cawed, then nothing. Now it was quiet. Perfectly quiet. Dead quiet.

"NICE JOB, GANG. I KNEW YOU COULD DO IT."

Yowzer! Big Voice.

HE was our client!

* 14 *

pay DIR+

The article was in the paper a few days later:

LA MALLE IS DEAD

Plans for La Malle, the eagerly awaited shopping center, have been canceled, a spokesperson for Double L Investments announced yesterday. This development was unexpected. "I know the folks in Grafton would have enjoyed these shops," said Neil Lamonde of Double L Investments. "But I've decided to allow the property to remain a cemetery. These people are my family. In my opinion, it's 'family first.'"

Mr. Lamonde also announced that he's leaving town. "I need to put in some quality me-time," he said in a phone interview from his new home in Manzanillo, Mexico.

"We did it!" yelled Kyle. "We shut out the shopping center."

"We solved the world's greatest case!" Lucy yelled. "And it wasn't Chuckie's scheme after all. We had a real, live client."

"*Braaaaack!*" squawked Scarface.

Call me crazy, but I'm the kind of detective who likes to dot all the i's and cross all the t's on a case. "Just a minute," I said. "A few things are still bothering me."

"Like what?" asked Kyle.

"Well, how did Big Voice find us? How did he know we were detectives?"

Kyle and Lucy shrugged.

"And another thing is Chuckie. I can't figure out why he wanted to hang with us. Was
it just to make money . . . or do you think it's
like he said about Neil? That he's not totally
rotten? Maybe he's trying to be nice? Maybe
he's lonely?"

"He hasn't even asked for his money yet. I
think Willie's right," Lucy said. "Maybe we
should feel sorry for him . . ."

"And let him join Scarface Detectives?!" I
asked.

Kyle shuddered. "Maybe Chuckie's not
totally rotten. But he mostly is."

Ding-dong. It was the doorbell. We answered it.

It was Chuckie. He didn't look that nice.

"Ahem," he said. He held out his big
hand. "Aren't you forgetting something?"

"Congratulations," I said, reaching out
carefully and then shaking his hand.

"Yeah yeah yeah," said Chuckie, dropping
my hand like a stone. "But I'm not after
thanks, I'm after the dough. You owe me,
big-time. If you don't pay now, I'm charging

interest. The clock is ticking. Tick tick tick—
ka-ching!"

"Oh." I smiled. Chuckie was back to being greedy and rotten. We didn't have to feel sorry for him!

Lucy asked, "How much is Chuckie's tab?"
I added it up:

Per diem charge (3 days @ $2.00) $6.00
Tree hole idea 1.00
Mongo info 5.00
    Total charge: $12.00

"It's twelve bucks," I said. Then we coughed up the dough.

Chuckie slid the money into his pocket.

"Thank you." He smiled his cheesy salesman smile. "It's been a real pleasure doing business with you." He reached into his pocket and pulled out some business cards. "You can pass these out to your friends."

The card said:

CHUCKIE'S BODYGUARD SERVICE
PROVEN RESULTS
REFERENCE: SCARFACE DETECTIVES

"I listed you as references," he said. "I hope you don't mind."

"Not at all," said Lucy. "We'd be happy to provide references. Let's say a dollar each?"

"You're gonna *charge* for a reference?" asked Chuckie.

"Each one. We *are* business people," I reminded him.

"*Ka-ching!*" said Scarface.

"Whatever," said Chuckie. "Well, anyway, I gotta be going. I have to think of how I'm going to invest my earnings. You know how it is with money. You snooze, you lose." And he took off.

"Good old Chuckie's back to being totally rotten," said Kyle. "So we don't have to let him join the agency!" He high-fived Lucy and me.

"And La Malle is history," said Lucy. "We even figured out that Big Voice was our client. Are we brilliant or what? Case closed. Now everybody can rest in peace."

But there were two more t's left uncrossed. "Let's go back to the cemetery, to have one last look around," I said.

* 15 *

MY DEAD FRIENDS

"It doesn't even feel creepy to stand on Loraine's grave anymore," I said.

"Yeah. It's like she's a friend now," said Lucy.

Scarface made her kissing noises, *"Mwiiip mwiiip mwiiip."*

"It doesn't even matter so much that we lost twelve dollars," Kyle said. "It was for a good cause. It's nice to know these dead guys don't have to move."

"YOU LOST TWELVE DOLLARS?" thundered a now-familiar voice. Our client.

"Yes," I said.

"WHERE DID YOU LOSE THE MONEY? BECAUSE IF IT WAS HERE, I COULD LOOK FOR IT." Big Voice walked from behind a bush. How long had he been standing there? Had he been hiding? Man, he really was weird.

"We hired Chuckie to be our bodyguard," Lucy said. "That's what he charged for protection."

"OHHH, THAT'S TOO BAD." Big Voice looked droopy and sad. Like melted plastic. "I DON'T LIKE MY FRIENDS TO LOSE MONEY."

"It's okay," I said. "It was for a good cause."

"TAKE THIS." Big Voice reached in his pocket and pulled out a ten and two ones.

"No, really," I said. "It's okay."

"I INSIST!" thundered Big Voice.

You don't argue with a guy that size. "Thanks," I said, taking the money.

"YOU KIDS REALLY DID A GOOD JOB.

I KNEW YOU COULD DO IT! I KNEW AS SOON AS I SAW YOUR POSTER."

So that's how Big Voice found us. The poster. Now there was just one more thing.

Big Voice grinned. "MY DEAD FRIENDS WILL BE HAPPY. THEY DON'T WANT TO MOVE."

"I know," Kyle said. "Nobody likes to move."

"MY DEAD FRIENDS AND I ARE GOING TO HAVE A PARTY NOW," Big Voice yelled. "TO CELEBRATE. WANNA COME?"

"Uh, no," said Lucy, looking at her watch. "We're late for, uh, an appointment. We have to go."

"OH. THAT'S TOO BAD." Big Voice had his melted-plastic face again. "BUT LORAINE WANTED YOU TO HAVE A REWARD."

Loraine?

Big Voice handed us a piece of paper. It was a gift certificate to the Chocolate Factory. For three Gigunda sundaes and one peanut butter sundae.

"THE GIGUNDAS ARE FOR YOU, AND THE PEANUT BUTTER SUNDAE IS FOR SCARFACE. LORAINE LO-O-O-OVES SCARFACE."

"*Loraine. Loraine. Mwiiip mwiiip mwiiip,*" said Scarface.

"CONGRATULATIONS ON THE CASE," yelled Big Voice, flapping his huge paw goodbye at us.

As we were leaving, Lucy said, "I'm glad it wasn't Chuckie's scam after all. I'm glad we had an actual client, even if he was a weirdo."

"I guess," I said. There was still that last t, though, the one that had me stumped. "But I was never really convinced it was Chuckie *or* Big Voice. I still have this skin crawly feeling, like maybe it really was the ghost of Loraine."

"Phooey," said Kyle. "I don't believe in ghosts. It's creepy fun to think about. But I think ghosts are just television stuff. They aren't real."

"Yeah," I said. "Anyway, we solved the world's greatest case. And my plan *was* brilliant."

Just then, somebody patted me on the back. "Thanks," I said to Kyle.

"For what?" he asked.

"Patting me on the back," I said.

"I didn't," he said.

"Lucy?" I asked. She shook her head no.

"Then who did?" I asked.

"*Loraaaaaine,*" said Scarface.

* About the Author *

Barbara M. Joosse is the author of four previous Wild Willie books and many other popular books for children, including the best-selling *Mama, Do You Love Me?* and *I Love You the Purplest*. She lives in Cedarburg, Wisconsin. You can learn more about Barbara M. Joosse at www.barbarajoosse.com.

* About the Illustrator *

Abby Carter has illustrated humorous books for children of all ages. Among her most recent chapter books are *Andy Shane and the Very Bossy Dolores Starbuckle* and *The Best Seat in Second Grade*. She lives in Hadlyme, Connecticut.